WELCOME TO CAMP CORAL!

By David Lewman

Based on the screenplay Tim Hill • Illustrated by Heather Martinez

 A GOLDEN BOOK • NEW YORK

© 2020 Paramount Animation, a division of Paramount Pictures, and Viacom International Inc. All rights reserved. Published in the United States by Golden Books, an imprint of Random House Children's Books, a division of Penguin Random House LLC, 1745 Broadway, New York, NY 10019, and in Canada by Penguin Random House Canada Limited, Toronto. Golden Books, A Golden Book, A Little Golden Book, the G colophon, and the distinctive gold spine are registered trademarks of Penguin Random House LLC. Nickelodeon, SpongeBob SquarePants, and all related titles, logos, and characters are trademarks of Viacom International Inc.

created by

Stephen Hillenburg

rhcbooks.com

T#: 689568

ISBN 978-0-593-12752-0

Printed in the United States of America

10 9 8 7 6 5 4 3 2 1

SpongeBob was SUPER EXCITED! His parents were dropping him off at Camp Coral, the greatest summer camp in the Seven Seas! He was going to have so much fun.

"If you're lucky, son," said his dad, "you'll come home with two of life's greatest gifts—friends and memories."

SpongeBob heard someone sobbing. He found a camper named Patrick crying because he was homesick.

"Maybe all you need is a friend," SpongeBob suggested.

"I don't HAVE any friends!" Patrick wailed. "BWAAAAH!"

"Well, you've got one now!" SpongeBob said cheerfully.

"Really?" Patrick said, sniffling. "Who is it?"

"It's me!" SpongeBob explained. "*I'll* be your friend!"

The new friends had all kinds of fun . . .
TOGETHER!

And Patrick forgot about being homesick.

While SpongeBob and Patrick were jellyfishing, a squirrel named Sandy floated down to the ocean bottom.

"Woo-hoo!" she whooped. "Hey, y'all critters of the sea! Look out below!"

SpongeBob introduced himself and Patrick. Sandy said she was from Texas and she liked to observe things, like underwater life, and report back to her sixth-grade classmates.

"You could be a scientist someday!" SpongeBob told her.

Sandy thought that was a great idea!

That night, there was a talent show. A counselor named Mrs. Puff said the campers would vote on the best performer. Whoever got the most votes would win the Campy Award!

Backstage, SpongeBob and Patrick
were getting ready to perform their act.
A camper named Squidward came in and
introduced himself.
Squidward was SURE his clarinet
playing would win him the Campy Award!

Mrs. Puff introduced Squidward. He walked onstage and started playing. He made strange shrieking noises on his clarinet.

everyone was confused by the weird music.
Some campers were even scared. Only SpongeBob
and Patrick clapped and cheered.

"Yay, Squidward!" they said.

"Thank you, thank you," said Squidward,
bowing. "Vote for me!"

SpongeBob and Patrick were up next. They sang a goofy song called "Aka Waka Maka Mia." It was about a pufferfish who wanted to be really big.

Patrick inflated SpongeBob until he was huge.
Then SpongeBob shot around the room like a
balloon losing air. He landed in another camper's
mouth. The camper spit SpongeBob out.

"Ta-da!" SpongeBob said, striking a pose.

Squidward laughed. "Terrible! The Campy
Award is mine for sure!"

But to Squidward's dismay, SpongeBob and Patrick won the Campy Award! Everyone clapped excitedly.

Squidward ran off crying. SpongeBob and Patrick looked at each other, worried about their new friend.

They found Squidward in his hut.
"Guess what, Squidward?" said SpongeBob.
"There was a big mistake! YOU won the Campy
Award!"
"I did?" Squidward asked, thrilled.
"Yep," Patrick said, handing him the award.
As Squidward hugged his prize, SpongeBob
winked at Patrick, who gave him a thumbs-up.

The next day, Mr. Krabs made
delicious Krabby Patties, following
his secret formula.

"You should open your own restaurant someday," SpongeBob told Mr. Krabs. "You could make a lot of money!"

"Money?" said Mr. Krabs. He liked SpongeBob's idea!

As SpongeBob walked away with his Krabby
Patties, Plankton tried to sell him food from
his Chum Mobile. The tiny chef complained that
everyone preferred the Krabby Patties.

"Why don't you ask Mr. Krabs for his secret
formula?" SpongeBob suggested.

"Good idea!" said Plankton. "I will!"

Plankton rushed to talk to Mr. Krabs.
SPLAT!
Thinking Plankton was a bug, Mr. Krabs swatted him with a frying pan.
"Jerk!" Plankton growled. "If it takes the rest of my life, I'll get you back for this!"

SpongeBob found a nice spot by the lake to eat his Krabby Patties. Just as he started to take a bite, he heard a meow.

He looked down and saw a little snail staring up at him.

Handing the snail a piece of food, SpongeBob asked, "What's your name?"

"Meow."

"Gary, huh?" SpongeBob said. "Well, hi, Gary! Do you want to be friends?"

"Meow!"

SpongeBob made lots of wonderful new friends and memories at Camp Coral. He thought it was the GREATEST CAMP EVER!